LET'S PLAY DDAKJI

Let's Play Ddakji

Brown Books Kids
Dallas / New York
www.BrownBooksKids.com
(972) 381-0009

A New Era in Publishing®

Publisher's Cataloging-In-Publication Data

Names: Im, Seo-Ha, author. | Jang, Joon-Young, illustrator.
Title: Let's play ddakji / Im Seo-Ha ; illustrated by Jang Joon-Young.
Description: Dallas ; New York : Brown Books Kids, [2022] | Audience: Ages 6-10. | Summary: It's vacation time! Woo
    is ready to visit his aunt, because that means he gets to play ddakji with his friends. Woo spent all year practicing
    and making the best ddakji-a bright, golden one. He made sure his was hard and heavy so he could beat Gorin, the
    reigning champion who won his ddakji last summer. When he loses to Gorin again, he makes it his mission to find the
    best material for his new ddakji so he can win. But Woo will find that a well crafted ddakji is only part of what it takes
    to win. The other? Fun! With this vibrant story about friendly competition, "Let's Play Ddajki" inspires kids to try a new
    game through Woo and Gorin's love of ddakji. Complete with colorful illustrations and detailed instructions on how
    to fold a ddakji, anyone can learn how to play this traditional Korean game from start to finish.--Publisher.
Identifiers: ISBN 9781612545837 (hardcover) | LCCN: 2022937818
Subjects: LCSH: Games--Korea--Juvenile fiction. | Friendship--Juvenile fiction. | Vacations—
Juvenile fiction. | Contests--Juvenile fiction. | Competition (Psychology) in children--Juvenile fiction. | Origami--Juvenile
    fiction. | Paper toys--Juvenile fiction. | Paper toy making--Juvenile literature. | CYAC: Games--Korea--Fiction. |
    Friendship--Fiction. | Vacations--Fiction. | Contests--Fiction. | Competition (Psychology)--Fiction. | Origami--Fiction.
| Paper toys-- Fiction. | Paper toy making. | BISAC: JUVENILE FICTION / Sports & Recreation / Games | JUVENILE
FICTION / Social Themes / Friendship.
Classification: LCC: PZ7.1.I377 L48 2022 | DDC: [E]--dc23

This book has been officially leveled by using the F&P Text Level Gradient™ Leveling System.

ISBN 978-1-61254-583-7
LCCN 2022937818

Printed in China
10 9 8 7 6 5 4 3 2 1

For more information or to contact the author, please go to
www.BrownBooksKids.com.

LET'S PLAY DDAKJI

Im Seo-Ha

Illustrated by Jang Joon-Young

BROWN BOOKS KIDS

"Hey, what are you doing? Aren't we playing ddakji now?" Minhae asked, but Woo didn't answer.

Woo thought to himself, *Ddakji should be made of paper! Plastic ddakji are no fun!*

He thought of last year when he played ddakji with Gorin.

If only I'd had a little stronger ddakji, I surely would have won. This summer I'll . . .

Suddenly, he got up and walked home.

"Woo! Over here!"

Woo found his mother standing at the school gate and ran toward her.

"Mom, let's go right now!"

"I'm glad that you're looking forward to seeing your aunt during vacation, even though you'll be away from home and me."

His mom seemed a little sad, but Woo didn't say anything. He was thinking only about ddakji.

After a long ride, they got to the community center of Hameupri, a rural village.

As soon as the car stopped, Woo got out and ran.

"Hey, son!" his mom called out, but Woo didn't answer. He just waved goodbye.

"Hello!" he shouted to the children who were
gathering in the backyard of the center.
They were very happy to see him again this year.
Woo said, "Let's play ddakji!"

At this, Gorin, who was standing behind the other children, said, "Kim Woo, you've come at last! We've been waiting for you."

    She sounded a little tough, but there was a smile on her face.

    Woo took out the ddakji he had brought, saying, "Wang Gorin! I'm going to win this time. You'll see."

    Full of confidence, he boasted, "Look! I made it. It's the strongest ddakji ever."

His new ddakji was glistening like gold and it was really thick and hard, which was perfect for playing ddakji.

"Wow! It's glittering like true gold!" the children exclaimed in amazement.

"OK. Let me play first!" Woo said excitedly.

Woo's ddakji won all the other children's ddakji with just one hit. It was king of the ddakji!

"Wow! This is absolutely the strongest ddakji ever!" the other children kept saying.

Encouraged by the adoration, Woo's hitting got more and more powerful.

"What do you think, Gorin? Isn't this the strongest ddakji you've ever seen?" Woo asked.

But Gorin said nothing and it made Woo more confident. He said, "Now, it's your turn. Hurry up and play!"

Gorin took out her old ddakji and shrugged.

"You know that when you lose the game, your ddakji will be mine, don't you?"

All the children were sure that Gorin would lose this time.

"OK, I'll hit first!"

Saying this, Woo threw down the golden ddakji with all his might.

At first, Gorin's ddakji seemed to tremble a little, but then, it didn't move any more.

"What happened? That's strange!" Woo said.

Woo hit once more, but Gorin's old ddakji still didn't flip over or even move.

"You're no match for me!"

Gorin threw down her ddakji without much power.

Woo couldn't believe his eyes as his golden ddakji flipped over!

Not only did his ddakji turn over, but so did everyone else's.

"This is ridiculous!" Woo exclaimed.

"Don't get upset!"

Though Gorin and the other children tried to comfort him, Woo said nothing and ran to his aunt's house.

"Not this paper!

"Or this one!

"None of these!"

Woo made ddakji after ddakji, folding every kind of paper and cardboard. He tried to remember what Gorin's ddakji was like, but it wasn't easy to make the same one.

I'm sure that the winning key is the ddakji itself, not her skill. There must be a secret to her ddakji, he thought to himself. He missed his golden ddakji, and he really wanted it back.

"I don't believe that she really meant to keep it. I'll go ask her to give it back to me."

Woo arrived at Gorin's house, but he didn't dare enter.

Her family ran a junk shop, which looked spooky at night. The heap of junk seemed to stare at him, and the ragged scarecrow was so frightening that Woo was ready to fight if it attacked.

Swish! Swinging a broken broomstick, Woo imagined himself fighting against a monster, when suddenly he heard a voice that terrified him.

"What are you doing?"

It was Gorin, but she looked like a ghost under the beam of the flashlight.

"Why didn't you come in? What are you doing with a broomstick?"

Gorin opened the door and let him in, tilting her head with curiosity.

Oh, what is all this? Woo thought to himself.

On the wall, there were lots of ddakji made of various colors and materials. The wall was practically papered with ddakji.

"Wow, a room made of ddakji!" Woo said.

While looking around at the ddakji, Woo found a familiar one.

"I used this one against you last year."

"Yeah, it's your silver ddakji. Do you remember when you said that it was the strongest ddakji ever?" Gorin said, smiling.

She had gotten nooroongji, a crispy rice crust, for them to eat from the kitchen.

Feeling embarrassed, Woo was looking at his silver ddakji when he found something written on it.
He found more writing on the ddakji next to it, too.
And on the next one!
Each ddakji had a name and a date on it.

Jin's Scribbled Ddakji, May 6, 2019
Woo's Strongest Silver Ddakji, August 3, 2019
Heejin's Cute Ddakji, June 3, 2018

Woo's Strongest Silver Ddakji

August 3, 2019

Heejin's Cute Ddakji

June 3, 2018

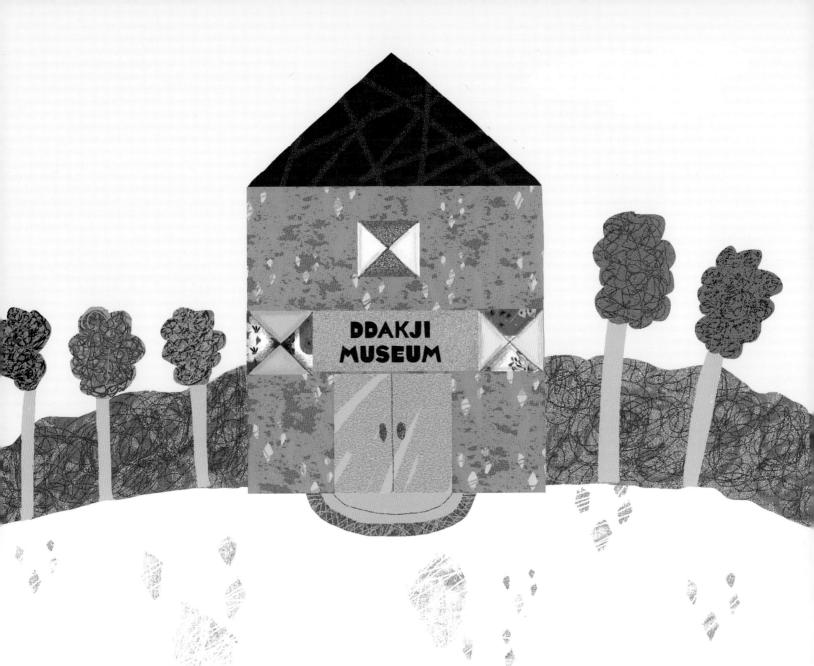

"I have a dream to build a ddakji museum," Gorin said.

"You don't want to be a ddakji champion, but open a ddakji museum?"

"Yeah, a place where we remember the happy times when we played the game together!"

Taking a big bite of nooroongji, she said, "Ddakji reminds me of my daddy."

Gorin brought out an old box with dust on it.
It was filled with various old ddakji.
"They were all made by my father when he was young," said Gorin.
"This one is made of a milk carton!" exclaimed Woo.
It was amazing to see all those ddakji made of different materials.
"Wow. This is the ddakji made from a picture of Robot Taekwon V.
My dad would tell me about it every day, but I have never seen it!"

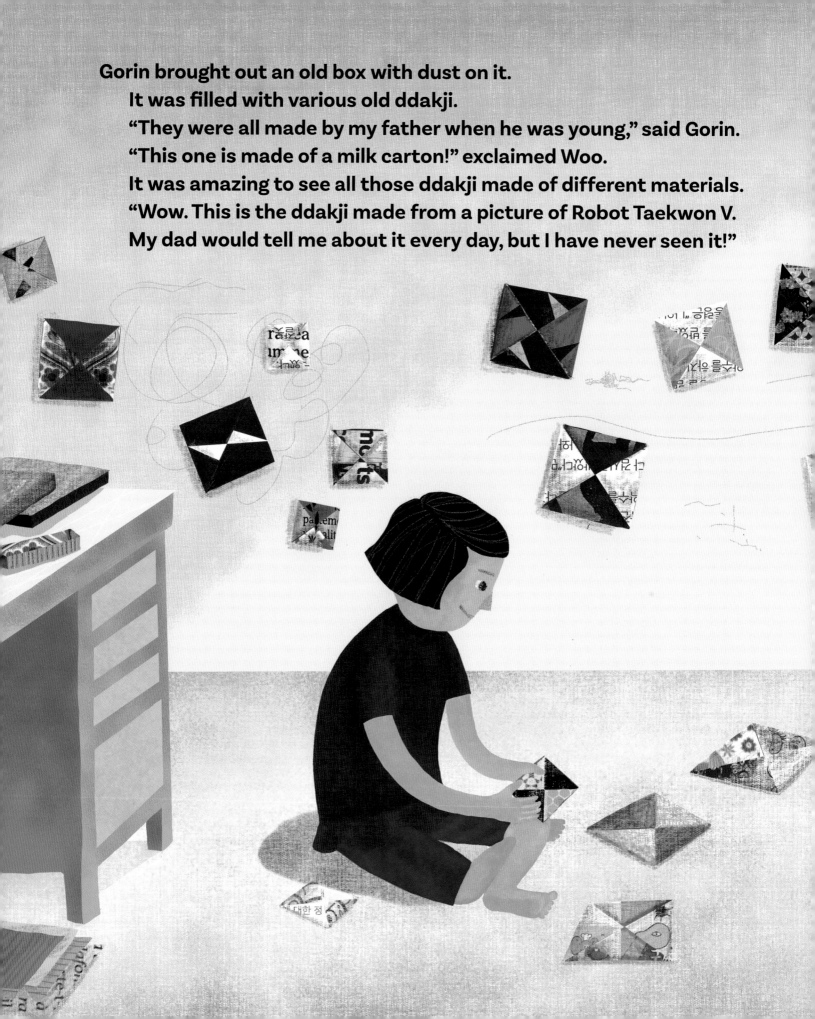

Gorin showed him a worn-out ddakji, the one she had used to win against him.

"Whenever I miss my father, I play ddakji. Then, I feel like I'm with him."

Woo now realized how Gorin looked while she was playing ddakji.

She looked truly happy and at ease!

That's because she felt like she was with her daddy who had passed away!

Who could ever win against a girl like that?

"I just wanted my ddakji back. But all this time, you've held on to every single ddakji because you've been dreaming of making a ddakji museum!"
Woo felt sorry about being angry with her.
"Woo, how about playing ddakji right now?"
Gorin challenged Woo with a bright smile.
"OK! But you should be ready to lose this time!"

What comes to your mind when you think of ddakji? You probably picture a plastic ddakji with a character on it, but in the old days, ddakji were not sold, so children had to make their own ddakji. Now, let's learn more about ddakjichigi.

The Origin of DdakjiChigi

It's not clear when ddakji were first created. In the very old days when paper wasn't easy to get, ddakji were made out of old book covers or old oiled floor paper. The shape is said to have been a trapezoid.

Around 1940, when paper became more available, children made square ddakji by folding paper. After the Korean War, quality paper started being produced and playing paper ddakji became very popular among children. Its popularity peaked between the 1960s to the 1980s but decreased from then until now, when not many children play with or even know about paper ddakji.

These days, plastic ddakji are sold with numbers or well-known cartoon characters on them, and children like to gather and play with them.

How to Fold a Ddakji

1) With one piece of paper

2) With two pieces of paper

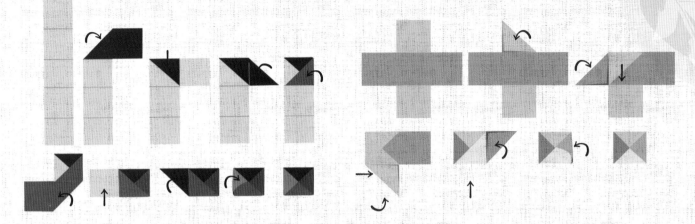

How to Play Ddakji

Ddakji is played by two or more players. The game starts when the first player throws down his/her ddakji either near or on the other ddakji. If any of the other ddakji turn over, the player who threw the ddakji wins and takes the overturned ddakji. Note that players are forbidden from making wind with a hand or sleeve.
It is called "wind-making" and it's against the rules.

There are two kinds of ddakji games. One is Gapan, which means that the game is not real, it's just for fun. In the Gapan game, the winner does not take the loser's ddakji. The other is Jinpan, which means that the game is real. In Jinpan, the winner takes the loser's ddakji. In order not to have a dispute with the other players, decide which kind of ddakji to play before starting a game.

1. Play rock paper scissors to decide who goes first. Everyone lays a ddakji on the ground except the winner of the rock paper scissors.

2. The first player throws down his/her ddakji with all his/her might so that the other ddakji may be flipped over.

3. If a player gets any of the other ddakji turned over, the player takes it and can keep playing. If a player's ddakji is overturned, that player must keep laying down another ddakji for the winner.

ABOUT THE AUTHOR

Im Seo-Ha studied literature at university. After graduation, she worked as an editor for a publishing house. Still, the chattering little writer in her heart kept sticking her head out and writing.

As an active co-creator of Three People—a creative group specializing in children's books—she has written many books, including *Let's Play Gonggidol, Let's Play Jeghi,* and *Pick and Read Traditional Fairy Tales from Textbooks.*

ABOUT THE ILLUSTRATOR

Jang Joon-Young majored in painting at both university and graduate school. She is inspired by the stories found in nature and the various stories of people. She strives to make picture books that warm the hearts of both children and adults.

Jang has written and illustrated books such as *What Kind of Sound Is This?, There Is a Road, Dinosaur Eggs and a Car,* and illustrated *What You Did From Sunrise Until Sunset?, My Grandfather Is a Fifteen-Year-Old Boy Soldier, Grandfather Candy Who Shares Love,* and *Come On!*

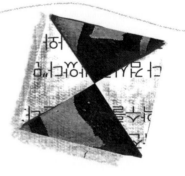